EXTREME CAREERS™

FRONTLINE MARINES

Fighting in the Marine Combat Arms Units

Simone Payment

rosen publishing's
rosen
central®

New York

Published in 2007 by The Rosen Publishing Group, Inc.
29 East 21st Street, New York, NY 10010

Library of Congress Cataloging-in-Publication Data

Payment, Simone.
Frontline Marines: fighting in the Marine combat arms units / Simone Payment.—1st ed.
p. cm.—(Extreme careers)
Includes bibliographical references and index.
ISBN-13: 978-1-4042-0946-6
ISBN-10: 1-4042-0946-8 (library binding)
1. United States. Marine Corps—Juvenile literature. 2. United States. Marine Corps—Vocational guidance—Juvenile literature. I. Title. II. Series.
VE23.P39 2006
359.9'631—dc22

                                                         2006010030

Manufactured in the United States of America

On the cover: A marine patrols an Iraqi checkpoint in 2004.

Contents

Introduction

Marines are known for their strength, bravery, and character. They are men and women of honor, courage, and commitment. They are trained to fight in wars, but they also serve their country by providing security and conducting humanitarian missions.

The marines who serve in the combat arms units are the troops on the ground, as opposed to the sea and sky. In this book you'll learn about the three units that make up the combat arms units: infantry, armor, and artillery. The jobs in these units are very dangerous, but they are also extremely exciting. Imagine this possible scenario in the life of a combat arms marine:

Suddenly, the quiet is broken by the sound of gunfire and explosions. Someone has fired on the combat arms marine troops that are out on patrol. It's time for their comrades to spring into action and fight back. Machine gunners and riflemen grab their weapons. Light armored vehicle crewmen start their vehicles. Field artillery cannoneers and mortarmen scramble for their ammunition.

Machine gunners then begin to shoot at enemy troops. Everyone stays alert. The combat arms marines know that danger is everywhere. There could be snipers on the roofs of buildings or loaded cannons hidden behind a burned-out truck. The troops talk to each other over their two-way radios, exchanging information and warnings.

One of the machine gunners spots enemy fighters trying to escape down an alley. Riflemen and machine gunners run after the enemy. They dart from one protected position to another. When they have a clear shot, the riflemen stop and fire. One of the enemy fighters goes down. After the marines hit another enemy fighter, the rest put down their weapons and come out with their hands raised in surrender.

Eventually, all the marines in the combat arms units return to base camp. They were lucky this time. Aside from a few troops with minor injuries, everyone is safe. They know that next time they might not be so lucky. However, the troops in this combat arms unit

A marine patrols the streets of Mosul, Iraq, from a Stryker. Strykers are light armored vehicles used in patrol and battle situations. They can reach speeds of 60 miles per hour (96.5 kilometers per hour).

know that they can count on each other because the U.S. Marine Corps demands excellence from its troops.

The three most important values in the U.S. Marines are honor, courage, and commitment. Marines are expected to follow these values at all times. They must honor each other as well as themselves. Marines must also be courageous in the face of extreme challenges. Finally, marines must be committed to the Marine Corps and to the United States.

The marines who serve in combat arms units are trained to be able to fight battles using their skills, their wits, and their trusty weapons. They face danger on a daily basis, never knowing for sure what they will encounter when they head off to battle. In the next few chapters you'll learn more about these marines. You'll also come to know the three groups that make up combat arms units.

The Combat Arms Units: An Overview

oday, marines are often the first troops to enter a conflict. They are trained to make their landings from the water. However, they have many other duties as well. The marines are a flexible, well-rounded fighting force. In addition to their battle duties, they provide security, take part in peacekeeping missions, and sometimes participate in special operations missions. Part of the security the marines provide is on naval bases around the world. They guard American embassies and government offices in other countries.

Another job the marines perform is humanitarian missions in the United States and around the world. During these operations, they help deliver food, water, and supplies to impoverished people. They also perform search-and-rescue missions during natural disasters such as floods, hurricanes, and earthquakes.

Here, a marine shakes hands with Liberian citizens in August 2003. The marines served at a port in Monrovia, Liberia, to help keep the peace in the country.

Sometimes marines serve in marine reconnaissance units. These highly trained units provide support to special operations forces (such as Army Rangers or Navy SEALs). At other times, marine reconnaissance units perform their own special operations missions. In these types of missions, they might rescue hostages or fighter pilots who have been shot down and captured by enemy forces. They might also blow up targets or perform scouting missions.

Working with the U.S. Navy

Although the Marine Corps is a separate military group, it works closely with the U.S. Navy. Both the navy and the marines are part of the Department of the Navy. Although the marines have their own aircraft, land vehicles, and troops, some marines serve on navy ships.

The Combat Arms Units

Each marine trains for a specific job. The jobs are called military occupation specialties (MOS). Several specialties are grouped together in units called combat arms. These units are on-the-ground fighting forces. They train in hand-to-hand combat, survival techniques, and weapons use.

The combat arms are made up of three units: infantry, armor, and artillery. Within each unit are specialties. In the infantry, marines can be riflemen, light armored vehicle crewmen, mortarmen, machine gunners, or anti-tank missile operators. In the armor unit, marines can be tank crewmen or amphibious assault vehicle (AAV) crewmen, which are crewmen who operate vehicles that can travel over both land and water. Field artillery radar operators, field artillery cannoneers, and field artillery fire control soldiers make up the artillery unit. You'll find more specific information on these specialties in the upcoming chapters.

Combat arms units marines work together in battle, so it's very important that they cooperate, take orders, and trust each other. Events unfold very quickly in battle, so as members of the combat arms units, marines must be able to think on their feet and adapt to changing conditions. They must depend on their brains as much as they depend on their weapons. Luckily, they can always rely on their training.

Training

Combat arms marines train hard from their first day of boot camp. In fact, training never really stops—they even continue to train during missions.

All combat arms marines begin their training at boot camp. Boot camp is a thirteen-week course of intense physical and mental preparation. The training is so

demanding that about one out of four recruits quits before finishing the course.

During boot camp, days are long. Recruits work from the moment they get up at 5:30 AM until they go

At Parris Island, South Carolina, female marine recruits undergo training. Though women aren't allowed into the combat arms units specifically, they do serve in other marine divisions.

to bed at 9:00 PM. They do physical drills like running and obstacle courses to increase strength and endurance. Marine recruits learn martial arts and other hand-to-hand combat skills. Recruits also learn

The Marine Motto: Semper Fidelis

In Latin, *semper fidelis* means "always faithful." Semper fidelis became the motto of the marines in 1883. It signifies the marines' commitment to America, to the Marine Corps, and to each other. Marines sometimes shorten the motto to semper fi and salute fellow marines with that message.

basic first aid and field cooking skills for life in the wilderness.

During boot camp, one of the most important things combat arms marines learn is how to use a rifle. They learn how to take apart and clean their rifles. They learn how the weapons work. When they know their rifles inside and out, the recruits learn how to shoot. Combat arms marine recruits spend hours performing shooting drills. They practice shooting at targets from various positions, such as kneeling or lying on the ground. Because gun battles sometimes take place in cities, recruits often practice on target ranges designed to look like cities, with buildings and alleys.

Combat arms marine recruits also practice reloading their rifles. It's important to be able to reload quickly in a firefight. Reloading can be difficult in battle conditions, when everything is happening fast. The more familiar they are with their weapons and ammunition, the better and faster the recruits will be at reloading.

Combat arms recruits who live east of the Mississippi River go to boot camp at Parris Island in South Carolina. Recruits from west of the Mississippi attend boot camp in San Diego, California. All female recruits go to a separate boot camp at the Parris Island location.

Near the end of boot camp, the combat arms marine recruits must endure what they call the Crucible. The definition of "crucible" is any type of severe test. This is the ultimate test of the skills of the combat arms marines. The Crucible lasts fifty-four hours. During that time, the combat arms marines do not eat or sleep. They perform rough physical tasks like a 40-mile (64-kilometer) march while wearing and carrying heavy equipment.

After boot camp, combat arms marines have two weeks off. They then go on to School of Infantry (SOI) training. During SOI, marine recruits who will be going into the infantry attend Infantry Training Battalion (ITB).

A Short History of the Marines

The American colonists formed the original U.S. Marines on November 10, 1775. The original marines fought during the Revolutionary War (1775–1783), in which the American colonies established their independence from Great Britain. After the war, the colonies formed their own government. The new government formally established the U.S. Marine Corps on July 11, 1798.

The marines fought many battles at sea during conflicts like the War of 1812 (1812–1814) and the Civil War (1861–1865). Later, the marines began to fight overseas as well.

They fought alongside army troops in World War I (1914–1918). During World War I, the slogan for the marines was "First to Fight." This is because the marines were often the first U.S. troops to enter a battle. Marines were trained to arrive by sea and then fight their battles on land. Launching from navy ships, they would land on a beach or riverbank. Once they were on the ground, they would attack enemy troops and fight them off. When the combat was underway, other U.S. troops could enter the battle and continue the fight.

The marines fought many long, hard battles in the Pacific during World War II (1939–1945), the Korean War (1950–1953), and the Vietnam War (1954–1975). They also fought in the Gulf War in Kuwait and Iraq in 1991. Most recently they have served in Afghanistan and Iraq.

A field artilleryman practices on a rifle range. He and his battalion are taking part in a two-day training program at the Camp Horno School of Infantry in California.

Recruits who will be in armor or artillery attend the Marine Combat Training Battalion (MCTBn).

When they are done with SOI, combat arms marines move on to specialized job training. Most specialty training lasts about eight weeks. However, some training may take as long as eighty weeks. When all training is complete, marines report for duty on a military base or a navy ship. There are about twenty bases in the United States and many others around the world.

The Infantry Unit

Imagine this scenario. It's the middle of the night and you're asleep in your tent. Awakened by the sound of someone shouting "Get on your gun!," you jump to your feet. You quickly gather your individual body armor (IBA) and run outside. You take your position behind your mortar tube and await your orders.

When the sergeant gives the call to fire your mortar, you are ready. Dropping a round of ammunition down the tube, you adjust the position of the gun. With the target coordinates locked in, you fire. You and your platoon continue to fire, sending off round after round. The shots light up the night sky while turning the target to rubble. With the enemy position destroyed, the sergeant calls "Cease fire." You're not quite done, though. First you must clean and reset your weapon. Then you prepare another stack of ammunition. You need to be ready in case you have to spring back into action. Now you are done and—maybe—you can go back to sleep.

This is an example of the life of the infantry in the marine combat arms units. The infantry is made up of troops who do battle on land. During combat, they close in on and destroy enemy forces. To do this, they use weapons and other military equipment. Sometimes, they use hand-to-hand combat. When necessary, they capture or kill enemy troops.

Infantry Duties: Preparing for Battle

The main duty of infantry troops is to prepare for battle ahead of the rest of the military. To prepare, marine infantry troops set up protection, including bunkers, barriers, and foxholes. After they have set up their protection, they sometimes disguise their positions with camouflage.

Infantry troops also prepare to fight by moving their weapons, ammunition, food, and water into the battle area. Depending on where the battle area is located, they might bring them in by land, sea, or air (they move

This marine pulls a member of his unit out of a bunker used for protection against incoming fire.

the supplies by air by parachuting them from a plane or releasing them from a helicopter).

Once their supplies and protection are in place, infantry troops make sure their weapons and other equipment are in good condition and ready to use. They clean their rifles and machine guns and stack their ammunition. They check their communications devices, such as two-way radios, to be sure they are in working order.

While preparing, infantry troops may also go on scouting missions to locate the enemy. They gather information about where enemy troops are located. They also pinpoint where the enemy's guns and equipment are positioned.

When their preparation duties are done, they wait for their battle orders. While they wait, they take part in drills to make sure their skills stay sharp. They continue their weapons training and practice their martial-arts skills. They may train in combat techniques such as surprise attacks or enemy capture.

Infantry Battle Duties

There are five specialties that make up the infantry unit of the combat arms units. The disciplines are: rifleman, light armored vehicle crewman, mortarman, machine gunner, and anti-tank missile operator. Each specialty has specific battle duties.

Riflemen

During boot camp, every combat arms marine spends hours learning how to use and care for a rifle. In fact,

U.S. Marine Corps Rifleman's Creed

Along with learning how to use and care for a rifle, marines learn the rifleman's creed. This is a statement that explains the importance of the rifle in the life of a marine. Here is an excerpt from the creed:

This is my rifle. There are many like it, but this one is mine. My rifle is my best friend. It is my life. I must master it as I must master my life. Without me my rifle is useless. Without my rifle, I am useless. I must fire my rifle true. I must shoot straighter than the enemy who is trying to kill me. I must shoot him before he shoots me.

the rifle is such an important piece of equipment to marines that one of their mottos is "Every marine a rifleman." Even if a marine someday becomes a general, he always considers himself a rifleman first.

The main rifle used by the marines is the M16A2 5.56 mm service rifle. The M16A2 is fired from the shoulder; this weapon is never fired from the hip, which is how it's often depicted in the movies. It can fire in single shots or can shoot three rounds at once as a semiautomatic weapon. The M16A2 can hit targets up to 2,625 feet (800 meters) away.

A marine training in Saudi Arabia is learning to use an M16A2 rifle, the standard rifle used in the infantry unit.

Although riflemen specialize in using rifles, they know how to use many other weapons, too. During battle, rifles are their main weapons. However, they may also use hand grenades and mines. They might use machine guns as well.

Mortarmen and Machine Gunners

The mortarman's main weapon is an M252 81 mm mortar. The M252 can shoot much farther than a rifle.

This mortarman is part of a crew that is fighting Iraqi insurgents in the Al Anbar province. He is adjusting the sights of his 81 mm mortar during a fire mission.

It can hit targets up to 3.5 miles (5.7 km) away. It is much heavier than a rifle and has to be set up on the ground and prepared by a crew of five before it can be shot.

The machine gunner uses several types of machine guns. All of them can fire many rounds of ammunition in a short amount of time. Like rifles, machine guns are fairly light and can be easily carried into battle.

Light Armored Vehicle and Anti-Tank Missile Operators

Light armored vehicle crewmen drive vehicles that are similar to tanks. They also operate machine guns that are mounted on the vehicles. Light armored vehicles have eight wheels. They can be driven in all kinds of weather and over the roughest terrain. They can reach speeds up to 62 mph (99 km/h) on land. When fully loaded for battle with ammunition and nine troops, they can weigh as much as 14.1 tons (12.8 metric tons).

An anti-tank missile operator specializes in using any of several anti-tank missiles, including the Dragon, the Javelin, and the tube-launched, optically tracked,

With their eight wheels, light armored vehicles can drive over almost any terrain. This makes them well suited to missions in rough terrain, such as the Iraqi desert.

wire-guided (TOW) missile. These missiles can destroy tanks or buildings and can be mounted on light armored vehicles. Some anti-tank missiles can be fired from a helicopter.

What It Takes to Join the Infantry

To join the infantry, recruits must be in excellent health and physical condition. Carrying heavy equipment over long distances requires that they are strong and have good endurance. They must be willing to face danger and extreme challenges. They also need to work well as part of a team. Each soldier must be able to rely on all the other soldiers in his unit. Excellent eyesight and hearing are also necessary for infantry positions. All five infantry positions are open only to men.

Some infantry positions have special requirements. For example, light armored vehicles can operate in water. Therefore, light armored vehicle crewmen must be strong swimmers. They must also have excellent driving records. In addition, for some jobs in the infantry, recruits must not be color-blind. This is because some of the weapons equipment is color-coded.

The Armor Unit

After Hurricane Katrina hit the Gulf Coast of the United States in 2005, the marine combat arms units arrived in the area to help victims. Some of the levees in New Orleans, Louisiana, had broken and much of the city was underwater. Amphibious assault vehicle (AAV) crewmen searched for residents trapped in the flood. For weeks, the combat arms crews crept through the polluted water with their AAVs.

The AAV can drive on land or right through water. The soldiers in New Orleans had to steer around fallen trees and abandoned cars, stopping to check every house and building. Sometimes they found people trapped inside the attic of a house. At other times, people flagged them down from the roofs of buildings where they went to escape the rising floodwaters.

Amphibious assault vehicles can be launched from ships and then travel effortlessly through water to shore, covering distances of up to 25 miles (40 km).

Marines took the rescued residents to safety, giving them food and water.

Armored assault vehicle crewmen drive tanks and other vehicles during and after disasters such as Katrina, as well as in military battles. Some operate tanks; others drive amphibious assault vehicles. Troops in the armor unit of the combat arms units help the infantry forces by protecting them from enemy fire and by firing on enemy targets themselves.

Armor Training

When recruits attend marine combat training battalion, they learn advanced battle techniques such as how to read maps and hide from the enemy. They also learn how to survive in harsh environments, like a scorching desert or snowy mountains.

When they complete battle training, marines who go into the armor unit get specialized armor training. During

One of the many important skills armor unit marines must learn is how to read maps. They must know how to quickly and accurately pinpoint their surroundings.

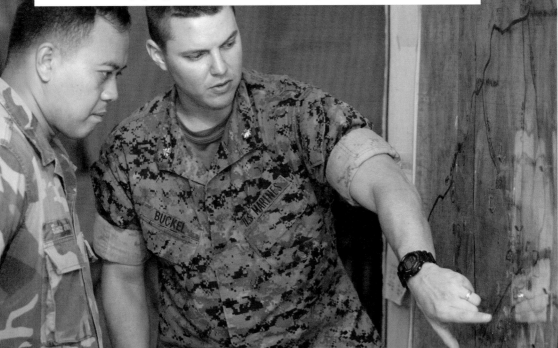

armor training, they learn how to drive and maintain armored vehicles. They learn to work with the guns and other weapons that are on the armored vehicles. Armor troops also learn how to track and locate enemy troops.

Armor Battle Duties

Before battle, armor troops help move infantry and artillery troops into battle areas. They also bring supplies into these areas. To prepare, they make sure their equipment is in good working condition. Armor troops sometimes help scout enemy positions. They may assist in preparing battle plans. When battle plans are in place, armor troops study the plans and read maps to get ready for battle.

There are two specialties that make up the armor unit of combat arms. The specialties are tank crewman and amphibious assault vehicle crewman. Although each specialty has specific duties, most of their duties are similar.

Tank Crewmen

Tank crewmen drive M1A1 tanks, which are armed with many types of guns. The M1A1 tanks weigh as much as

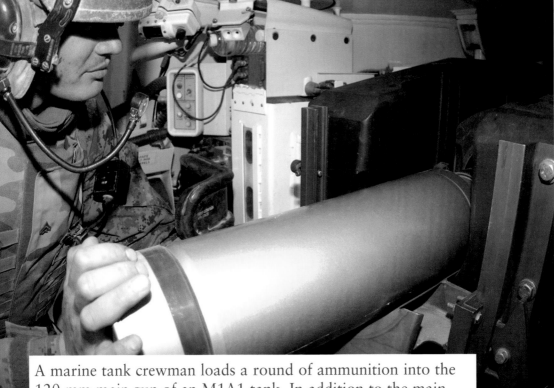

A marine tank crewman loads a round of ammunition into the 120 mm main gun of an M1A1 tank. In addition to the main gun, M1A1 tanks are also armed with several machine guns.

68 tons (62 metric tons). Tank crewman load and fire the weapons mounted on the tank. They also operate the communication equipment in the tank. This allows them to talk with other vehicle drivers and to get orders about the battle plans. During missions they use computerized equipment in the tank to read maps and keep up with battle plans.

Before and after battles, tank crewmen take care of their vehicles. If necessary, they make repairs or do other maintenance.

Amphibious Assault Vehicle Crewmen

Like tank crewmen, amphibious assault vehicle crewmen drive vehicles and fire weapons. However, the vehicles they drive can also operate in water. Amphibious assault vehicles can carry up to twenty-five combat arms marines. They are covered with armor and have machine guns for defense. They can travel as fast as 45 mph (72 km/h) over land. In water, they can usually go about 6 to 8 mph (9.6 to 12.9 km/h). Because AAVs can travel in water, they bring supplies and troops from ships to shore. They can also be used in battle.

Amphibious assault vehicle crewmen maintain and repair their AAVs. They also operate and maintain weapons and communication equipment.

What It Takes to Join the Armor Unit

Armor troops must be in good health and top physical condition. Space inside armored vehicles is limited, so armor troops must be able to be comfortable in small spaces for long periods of time. Because of the limited

Marine Corps Oath

When recruits join the marines, they make a pledge to serve the marines and the United States. Here is the oath all marines must make:

> I do solemnly swear (or affirm) that I will support and defend the Constitution of the United States against all enemies, foreign and domestic; that I will bear true faith and allegiance to the same; that I will obey the orders of the President of the United States and the orders of the officers appointed over me, according to regulations and the Uniform Code of Military Justice. So help me God.

space inside vehicles, armor crew must work well with other people. In stressful, dangerous conditions, armor troops must remain calm and keep a clear head.

Armor crewmen must have good driving skills. They can't be color-blind because maps and some equipment, ammunition, and computer displays are color-coded. Amphibious assault vehicle crew members must also be strong swimmers.

The Artillery Unit

O n a typical day for a soldier in the artillery unit of the combat arms units, explosions are rocking the ground and the troops in the unit are scrambling to get to their shooting positions. Staying calm, they quickly read the information coming in to their computers. They get coordinates from the radar system, which tell them the enemy's shooting positions. The coordinates are yelled out to the mortarman. Loading his mortar, he quickly returns fire. Within minutes, the enemy has been taken out. Soon, all is quiet again.

Combat arms marines in the artillery unit protect and support the infantry and armor troops. They do this by defending the troops from enemy attacks. They also fire on the enemy, destroying enemy troops, weapons, and equipment.

The AN/PSN-11 is a small handheld Global Positioning System (GPS). It allows marines to send and receive accurate information about their positions and those of their enemies.

Artillery Training

After marine combat training battalion, combat arms marines who join the artillery unit get additional training that is tailored to what they want to specialize in. This training lasts from ten to fourteen weeks. The length of the course depends on what specialty a recruit chooses. During training, recruits learn to use computerized

Marines: Gung-ho

Members of the artillery team have to work together to get things done. Like every combat arms marine, they have a positive attitude that they call "gung-ho." "Gung-ho" is a Chinese phrase that means "working together." The Chinese first used "gung-ho" to refer to the marines around 1900. They noticed that the marines worked well together. The term still describes the marines today.

systems to locate targets, how to handle ammunition, and how to load and fire the specialized equipment they will use on the battlefield.

Artillery training takes place in the classroom and in the field. Like boot camp, troops train hard in all kinds of conditions. This helps prepare them for any situation they might face during their duties. Some artillery crews serve on ships, so recruits do additional training at sea.

Artillery Duties: Preparing for Battle

The artillery unit is always preparing for battle. They keep their ammunition in order, making sure the ammunition stays dry and neatly arranged. Ammunition must be easily found by troops, as they will need to be able to locate it during the chaos of battle.

Weapons are also cleaned frequently to keep them in good working order. Artillery crewmen know how to take each weapon apart and then put it back together. The artillery units also use other types of gear, like computerized target equipment. They must keep this equipment in good shape as well.

Artillery Battle Duties

There are three specialties that make up the artillery unit of the combat arms units. The specialties are field artillery radar operator, field artillery cannoneer, and field artillery fire control man. Each specialty has specific battle duties.

Field Artillery Radar Operators

As the title describes, field artillery radar operators specialize in working with radar equipment. This equipment tracks the position of enemy troops. It also detects enemy fire. Combat arms artillery marines use a Q36 or Q37 radar. The Q36 is used to locate incoming

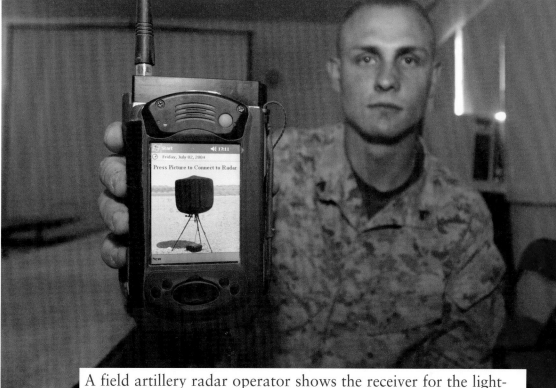
A field artillery radar operator shows the receiver for the light-weight counter mortar radar system. This small device shows the coordinates of enemy mortar equipment.

short-range, low-velocity weapons such as mortars and artillery. The Q37 is designed to locate long-range, high-velocity weapons such as rockets. The radar operator can then relay the information to the other troops. This allows the troops to avoid the enemy fire and fire back at the enemy position.

When they are not tracking enemy fire, field artillery radar operators take care of the equipment. After all, everyone depends on it as an early warning system. They also prepare the equipment for transport.

The 155 mm Howitzer cannon can be brought into battle position by helicopter or towed by tank. It can fire accurately at long distances, which makes it a valuable weapon.

Field Artillery Cannoneers

A field artillery cannoneer works as part of the team that sets up and fires huge cannons. The cannons are used to destroy large, stationary targets, such as enemy bunkers and buildings. To fire the weapon, the field artillery cannoneer and the rest of the team must load it with ammunition. Then they pack it with gunpowder, close it, add a detonator, aim it, and fire. One team member keeps track of whether the target was hit. If the first round misses the target, the team reloads the cannon and fires again.

One weapon that a field artillery cannoneer might use is a 155 mm Howitzer cannon. It takes seven men to set up, load, and fire the Howitzer. This weapon can shoot accurately up to 18 miles (30 km). It weighs about 7.6 tons (7.2 metric tons).

In addition to firing the cannon, a field artillery cannoneer and other team members are responsible for moving the cannon. When they get it to the specified location, they prepare the area, making sure the ground is level so the cannon will fire straight. Sometimes the team will camouflage the cannon so it can't be spotted by the enemy. The field artillery cannoneer also keeps the cannon and ammunition clean. In addition, he performs routine maintenance and makes small repairs.

Field Artillery Fire Control Men

Working with other members of the artillery team, field artillery fire control men make sure weapons will hit their targets. They use computers and other tools to locate targets and set up weapons to hit them. When weapons, like cannons, are fired, a team member keeps track of where the ammunition hit. The field artillery control man uses that data to reset artillery for the next shot. Field artillery control men also help other artillery team members set up, maintain, test, and repair equipment.

What It Takes to Join the Artillery Unit

Just like infantry and armor troops, artillery troops must be strong and healthy. They must be able to work for long periods of time without rest. They must also be able to stay calm and keep a clear head in stressful combat situations. Finally, they must work well with others and be brave in the face of extreme danger.

Some artillery jobs require good computer and math skills. Artillery crewmen can't be color-blind. This is because they need to read maps and see colors on equipment, ammunition, and computer displays.

Serving in the Combat Arms Units

Do you think you would like to join the combat arms units of the marines? To join the marines, you must have a high school degree. You must be between eighteen and twenty-eight years old. (You may join the marines at seventeen years old, but must have signed permission from a parent.) You must be in excellent health and physical condition. Also, you must be a U.S. citizen or a legal U.S. resident.

Before you can join, you must pass the Armed Services Vocational Aptitude Battery test (ASVAB). It tests a potential recruit's math and reading skills, and other skills such as knowledge of electronics or auto repair. The test also helps match a recruit to the right job within the marines. For example, if you score well in the math area of the test, your recruiter might suggest

To improve scores on the Armed Services Vocational Aptitude Battery (ASVAB) test, active-duty marines can take part in the Military Academic Skills Program (MASP).

several jobs that involve math that you might be good at and enjoy.

If you join the combat arms units of the marines, or the marines in general, you must sign a contract that binds you to stay for four years. After that, if you'd like to continue in the marines, you can sign a new contract for two, three, or four more years.

"A Few Good Men" ... and Women

The marines have very high standards for who can join. They are always looking for "a few good men." Marine captain William Jones first used this expression in 1779. He was recruiting men to join the marines in Boston, Massachusetts.

Although jobs in combat arms units are not open to women, women can serve in many other jobs in the marines. They can be engineers, aircraft mechanics, drivers, and combat pilots.

Women first served in the marines in World War I. However, they could only serve in office jobs and not on active duty. In 1948, women were allowed into the marines in active-duty positions.

Benefits

There are many benefits to joining the marine combat arms units. The Marine Corps pays for recruits' food, health care, and housing while they are on duty. In addition, marines are paid for their service. Salary is based on the level of your position and your years of service. The marines also factor in hardship pay if you are serving overseas or in a particularly dangerous job. The lowest base pay for 2006 was $28,738. In addition, the marines can help you pay for college after finishing service. They may also help pay college loans if you have gone to college before you begin serving.

The Reserves

If you decide you don't want to serve in the marine combat arms units on a full-time basis, consider joining the Marine Reserves. As part of the reserves, you work one weekend per month. In addition, you work two full weeks during the year, usually during the summer. Serving in the Marine Reserves allows you to attend college or work full time. However, during a war, you must agree to serve full time on active duty.

The Marine Reserves have the same requirements for joining as the regular marines. Reserves go through the same training and have the same benefits while they serve on active duty.

Preparing for Duty

If you'd like to join the marine combat arms units, there are a few things you can do to prepare. First of all, it's important to stay in school. Remember that you must have a high school degree to join.

Recruiters can provide information about all aspects of life in the marines. They can also help recruits prepare to take the ASVAB test and to get ready for basic training.

Talk to your school guidance counselor or a marine recruiter. They can give you more specific information about careers in the marine combat arms units or other military branches.

Until it is time to join the marine combat arms units, you can prepare physically by getting your body in good shape. Start conditioning exercises such as running. You can also do strength training such as lifting weights. Eat a healthy, balanced diet. Make sure to drink plenty

Famous Marines

Many men and women go on to rewarding careers in civilian jobs after serving in the marines. Here are a few well-known former marines who have gone on to do great things in a variety of fields:

1. **David Dinkins**, the first African American mayor of New York City
2. **John Glenn**, astronaut, U.S. senator
3. **Gene Hackman**, Oscar-winning actor

of water and other fluids, especially when you are training during the summer months.

Exercise and good nutrition help take care of your body and can also improve your mental strength. In addition, you may want to consider joining team sports or organizations. Participating in unit activities can build leadership skills and teamwork. Both of these are essential to being a good combat arms marine.

Although serving in a combat arms unit can be dangerous, it can also be rewarding. Marines learn many valuable life skills during their training and service. These skills serve them well in their later years.

Glossary

ammunition Bullets or other lethal objects (such as explosives) fired from weapons.

amphibious Able to be used on both land and water.

artillery Large weapons, or a part of the military that uses large weapons.

battalion A military unit made up of two or more smaller units.

bunker A shelter dug into the ground to withstand an attack.

camouflage Hiding or disguising something by changing the way it looks; the material or clothing used to disguise something.

character Moral standing.

civilian A person not on active duty in the military.

coordinates A set of numbers used to locate a point on a map.

embassy The house or office of an ambassador in a
   foreign country.

fortification A construction built for defense.

foxhole A pit in the ground used to take cover from
   an enemy.

humanitarian Describes providing help or aid to
   someone in need.

infantry Soldiers trained and armed to fight on foot.

levee A structure built along a river to prevent flooding.

maintenance Taking care of property or equipment.

mortar A short cannon used to fire shells.

motto A short expression of a guiding rule of conduct.

primer A device that contains an explosive that will set
   off a larger explosive.

reconnaissance A survey of enemy territory to gather
   information about the opponent.

For More Information

Marine Corps Division of Public Affairs
Headquarters Marine Corps
3000 Marine Corps
Pentagon 4A532
Washington, DC 20350-3000
(703) 614-1034/1054
Web site: http://www.marines.mil/pashops/
pashops.nsf/pamain

**Marine Corps Recruit Depot/
Eastern Recruiting Region**
Parris Island, SC 29905
(843) 228-2111
Web site: http://www.mcrdpi.usmc.mil/index.htm

Marine Corps Recruit Depot/
Western Recruiting Region

1600 Henderson Avenue

San Diego, CA 92140

(619) 524-1011

Web site: http://www.mcrdsd.usmc.mil

Marines Magazine

Superintendent of Documents

U.S. Government Printing Office

Washington, DC 20402

(888) 293-6498

Web site: http://www.mcnews.info/mcnewsinfo/
marines/gouge/

Parris Island Museum

P.O. Box 5202

Parris Island, SC 29905

(843) 228-2951

Web site: http://www.mcrdpi.usmc.mil/units/museum/
index.htm

Women Marines Association
P.O. Box 8405
Falls Church, VA 22041-8405
Web site: http://www.womenmarines.org

Web Sites

Due to the changing nature of Internet links, the Rosen Publishing Group has developed an online list of Web sites related to the subject of this book. This site is updated regularly. Please use this link to access the list:

http://www.rosenlinks.com/ec/froma

For Further Reading

Bartlett, Merrill L., and Jack Sweetman. *The U.S. Marine Corps: An Illustrated History*. Annapolis, MD: Naval Institute Press, 2001.

Benson, Michael. *The U.S. Marine Corps*. Minneapolis, MN: Lerner Publishing Group, 2005.

Cooper, Jason. *Marine Corps: Fighting Forces*. Vero Beach, FL: Rourke Publishing LLC, 2004.

Flach, Andrew. *The United States Marine Corps Workout*. Long Island City, NY: Hatherleigh Press, 2004.

Harmon, Daniel E. *The U.S. Armed Forces*. Philadelphia, PA: Chelsea House Publishers, 2001.

Keeter, Hunter. *The U.S. Marine Corps*. Milwaukee, WI: World Almanac Library, 2005.

Kennedy, Robert C. *Life in the Marines*. New York, NY: Children's Press, 2000.

Rowan, N. R. *Women in the Marines: The Boot Camp Challenge.* Minneapolis, MN: Lerner Publishing Group, 1994.

Voeller, Edward A. *U.S. Marine Corps Special Forces: Recon Marines.* Mankato, MN: Capstone Books, 2000.

Bibliography

"Armored Assault Vehicle Crew Members."
    TodaysMilitary.com. January 27, 2006. Retrieved
    January 30, 2006 (http://www.todaysmilitary.com/
    app/tm/careers/combatspecialty/enlisted/
    armoredassaultvehiclecrewmembers).

"Artillery and Missile Crew Members." TodaysMilitary.com.
    Retrieved January 24, 2006 (http://www.todaysmilitary.
    com/app/tm/careers/combatspecialty/enlisted/
    artilleryandmissilecrewmembers).

"Artillery Marines Return to Firing." Marines.com.
    Retrieved January 24, 2006 (http://www.usmc.mil/
    marinelink/mcn2000.nsf/main5/E1165BF2F2FC55C
    E8525710300668BF2?opendocument).

Benson, Michael. *The U.S. Marine Corps*. Minneapolis,
    MN: Lerner Publishing Group, 2005.

Hacker, Corporal Matthew K. "2nd Supply Battalion Trains Its Marines for the Inevitable." Marine Corps News. January 23, 2006. Retrieved January 25, 2006 (http://www.marines.mil/ marinelink/mcn2000.nsf/main5/ A41BBD7B16A0FEA5852570FF006EE6F3? opendocument).

Halasz, Robert. *The U.S. Marines.* Brookfield, CT: The Millbrook Press, 1993.

Harmon, Daniel E. *The U.S. Armed Forces.* Philadelphia, PA: Chelsea House Publishers, 2001.

"Infantry." TodaysMilitary.com. Retrieved January 24, 2006 (http://www.todaysmilitary.com/app/tm/ careers/combatspecialty/enlisted/infantry).

Keeter, Hunter. *The U.S. Marine Corps.* Milwaukee, WI: World Almanac Library, 2005.

Miller, Lance Corporal Peter R. "Mortarmen Support Infantry Near Hit, Iraq." Marine Corps News. January 17, 2006. Retrieved January 26, 2006 (http://www.usmc.mil/marinelink/mcn2000.nsf/ 0/227f0e35e36dfadf852570f9003b938c? OpenDocument).

Mortenson, Darrin. "Iraqis Strike Back: Street Fighters Ambush Marine Advance into Fallujah." *North County Times*. April 6, 2004. Retrieved January 26, 2006 (http://www.nctimes.com/articles/2004/04/06/military/iraq/0_0_5_0412_10_16.%20%20%20%20%20%20%20%20%20%20%20%20txt).

"My Rifle: The Creed of a United States Marine." United States Marine Corps History and Museums Division. Retrieved January 26, 2006 (http://hqinet001.hqmc.usmc.mil/HD/Historical/Frequently_Requested/Marines%27_Rifle_Creed.htm).

Nevers, Captain David. "Help for the Homeland: 24th Marine Expeditionary Unit Delivers Hurricane Relief." *Marines*, Vol. 34, No. 4, October–December 2005. Retrieved January 25, 2006 (http://www.mcnews.info/marines/fromthetrenches/helphomeland.shtml).

Rhodes, Corporal Shawn C. "New Radar System Brings the Fight Back to Terrorists." Marine Corps News. July 3, 2004. Retrieved January 26, 2006

(http://www.usmc.mil/marinelink/mcn2000.nsf/0/
835bbd0217b5de3285256fea005cb4e2?
OpenDocument&Highlight=2,lcmr).
Warren, James A. *American Spartans: The U.S. Marines,
A Combat History from Iwo Jima to Iraq.* New York,
NY: Free Press, 2005.

Index

About the Author

Simone Payment's title *Inside Special Operations: Navy SEALs* (also from Rosen Publishing) won a 2004 Quick Picks for Reluctant Young Readers award from the American Library Association and is on the Nonfiction Honor List of Voice of Youth Advocates. She has a degree in psychology from Cornell University and a master's degree in elementary education from Wheelock College. She is the author of fifteen books for young adults, several of which are about the military.

Photo Credits

Cover © Justin Sullivan/Getty Images; p. 6 © Chris Bouroncle/AFP/Getty Images; p. 9 © Chris Hondros/Getty Images; pp. 12–13, 48 © Scott Olson/Getty Images; p. 17 Lance Cpl. Ray Lewis, MCB Camp Pendleton, USMC; p. 20 © Nicolas Asfouri/AFP/Getty Images; p. 23 Lance Cpl. Eric R. Lowndes, 26th MEU. USMC; p. 24 Sgt. Richard D. Stephens, 22nd MEU, USMC; p. 26 Pfc. Michael S. Cifuentes, MCAGCC, USMC; p. 29 Lance Cpl. Mich\elle M. Dickson, USMC; p. 30 Lance Cpl. Scott M. Bisculti, MCB Camp Pendleton, USMC; p. 32 Gunnery Sgt. Rob Blakenship, 11th MEU, USMC; p. 36 Cpl. Veronika Tuskowski, 1st Marine Division, USMC; p. 39 Cpl. Shawn C. Rhodes, 1st Marine Division, USMC; p. 40 Cpl. Christopher Korhonen, MCB Camp Butler, USMC; p. 45 Lance Cpl. Christopher Roberts, MCB Quantico, USMC; p. 49 (left) © Lawrence Lucier/Getty Images; p. 49 (middle) Bill Ingalls/NASA via Getty Images; p. 49 © (right) Evan Agostini/ Getty Images.

Editor: Nicholas Croce